ad Book™

and Moo

The Night of
the Living Bed

Den s
Cazet
y

HarperCollins*Publishers*

For
Margot
and the boys—
Leo, Christopher, and Nicholas

HarperCollins®, ☙®, and I Can Read Book® are
trademarks of HarperCollins Publishers Inc.

Minnie and Moo: The Night of the Living Bed
Copyright © 2003 by Denys Cazet
Manufactured in China. All rights reserved.
For information address HarperCollins Children's Books,
a division of HarperCollins Publishers,
10 East 53rd Street, New York, NY 10022.
www.harperchildrens.com

Library of Congress Cataloging-in-Publication Data
Cazet, Denys.
   Minnie and Moo : the night of the living bed / Denys Cazet.
      p.   cm. — (An I can read book)
   Summary: Minnie's barnyard friends find a way to make her feel better
when a bad dream upsets her and sends her bed rolling into town on
Halloween night.
   ISBN 0-06-000503-3 — ISBN 0-06-000504-1 (lib. bdg.)
   ISBN 0-06-000505-X (pbk.)
   [1. Halloween—Fiction. 2. Dreams—Fiction. 3. Cows—Fiction.
4. Domestic animals—Fiction. 5. Humorous stories.] I. Title: Night of the
living bed. II. Title. III. I can read book.
PZ7.C2985 Mmo 2003   2002152612
[E]—dc21   CIP
                                                                                     AC

10   11   12   13   SCP   10   9   8
❖

The Dream

The Halloween moon

rose behind the old oak tree.

Far away, a dog howled.

Minnie tried to sleep.

She tossed and turned.

Strange dreams came and went.

One dream wouldn't go away.

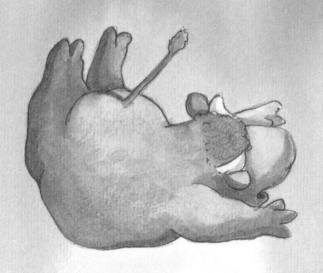

In the dream, a giant mouse

ate the last bit of chocolate

in the whole world.

"Nooooooo," Minnie moaned.

The giant mouse laughed.

Then, he ate the last cream puff.

"NOOOOOOOOOO!" Minnie shouted.

Minnie grabbed Moo.

"Mine!" she yelled, shaking Moo.

"Spit it out, you rat! Spit it out!"

They rolled off the bed.

"Help!" Moo shouted.

"Minnie! Wake up!"

The Living Bed

Minnie woke up.

"You had a bad dream," said Moo.

Minnie sighed.

"The world was without chocolate,"

she said. "A giant mouse ate it."

Moo put her arm around Minnie.

"It was only a dream," said Moo.

9

"Everything is fine."

"No, it isn't," said Minnie. "Look!

Our bed is rolling down the hill!"

"It must have started to roll

when we fell out!" cried Moo.

"Catch it!"

Minnie and Moo ran after the bed.

When they caught up to it,

they jumped on the back.

The bed rolled faster.

"Hang on!" yelled Minnie.

The bed raced through the barn.

It scooped up two sheep

and Hamlet, the pig.

"Look out!" shouted Moo.

12

The bed scooped up Madge
and Bea Holstein.

It whizzed out the back of the barn
and zoomed down the hill.

13

It shot up another hill

and rolled into town.

It squeaked to a stop

in front of a sign

that said Bus Stop.

Treats

The animals climbed off the bed.

Madge put her hooves on her hips.

"What was THAT about?" she asked.

"One minute we're asleep in the barn

and the next we're awake

in the street!" said Bea.

"What happened?" Hamlet asked.

Everyone looked at Moo.

"Well . . . " said Moo.

"It wasn't Moo's fault," said Minnie.

"It was mine.

I had a bad dream.

We fell out of bed.

The bed rolled down the hill

and here we are."

Minnie sniffed.

"In my dream a giant mouse

ate my last cream puff."

"Ohhh!" Bea and Madge gasped.

They hugged Minnie tightly.

"You poor, poor thing," said Madge.

Two little ghosts walked by.

"Trick or treat," they said.

Moo waved at the little ghosts.

"Treats," said Bea. "That's the way
to chase away a bad dream."

"Chocolate is the best," said Madge.

"We don't have any chocolate,"
said the sheep.

"Or any treats," said Hamlet.

Moo watched the two little ghosts
walk up to a big white house.

"That's it!" said Moo.

"I know where we can get

some treats . . . chocolate treats!"

"Really?" said Minnie.

Moo handed Madge and Minnie

each an empty pillowcase.

"Really," said Moo. "Follow me."

Cows Go Moo

The animals walked up

to the door of the big white house.

Moo rang the doorbell.

A man opened the door.

"Wow!" he said. "Look at you kids.

You look like real farm animals."

The man looked at Moo.

"What's your name, kid?"

"Moo," said Moo.

"I know cows go moo," said the man.

"But what's your name?"

"Moo," said Moo.

The man looked at Minnie.

He held up a candy bar.

"Now," he said,

"tell me your friend's name."

"Moo," said Minnie.

"Very funny," said the man.

He looked at the other animals.

"Who would like the rest

of this candy?" he asked.

All the animals raised their arms.

"Okay," said the man.

"Tell me the name of the kid

in that cow suit."

"Moo," said Madge.

"Moo," said Bea.

"Moo," said Hamlet.

"Moo," said the sheep.

25

"Kids!" said the man.

He closed the door

and turned off the porch light.

Tricks

They walked to the next house.

"Maybe you have to do a trick first,

and then you get a treat," said Moo.

"I'll be first," said Minnie.

She rang the doorbell.

A lady opened the door.

Minnie jumped up and down.

She jumped faster and faster.

Then she stopped

and held out her bag.

"Must be that Johnson kid,"

the lady muttered.

She put a candy bar in the bag
and closed the door.

Everyone looked at Minnie.

"That was my trick," she said.

"I was being a milk shake."

They walked to the next house.

"My turn," said Hamlet.

"I know a really good trick."

Hamlet found a hose

and filled his mouth with water.

Moo rang the bell.

When a man opened the door,

Hamlet sang the song "Glow Worm"

and gargled at the same time.

"Kids," muttered the man.

He dumped candy into both bags
and closed the door.

More Tricks

At each house someone did a trick.

At one of the last houses,

Madge stood upside down on the lawn

and balanced on one horn.

The horn poked a hole in a pipe

and water shot up into the air.

Everyone got soaked.

The sheep swelled up

to three times their size.

Moo rang the bell

and a lady answered.

"Goodness," she said.

"Four cows, a pig, and, and . . ."

The lady looked at the sheep.

"Don't tell me!" she said.

"I know! Sponges! Four cows, a pig,

and two walking sponges!

You children are so clever."

The lady filled the bags with candy.

"Now run along home," she said.

"And get into some dry clothes."

The lady looked up into the night.

"Isn't that strange?" she said.

"It's raining

and there isn't a cloud in the sky."

She closed the door.

"This bag is full," said Madge.

Minnie looked into her bag.

"Mine too," she said.

"Isn't it beautiful?"

Bus Service

When they got back to the bus stop,

they found a little old lady

standing on the bed.

"Well!" she said. "It's about time!"

The lady gave Moo a bus token.

"Drop me off at Fifth Street."

Moo stared at the lady.

"Well?" the old lady said,
rapping the bed with her cane.
"Get this bus moving!"
"Moo!" gasped Minnie, pointing
across the street. "LOOK!"

A huge mouse was walking

toward them, carrying a big bag.

"IT'S HIM!" Minnie shouted.

"SAVE THE CHOCOLATE!

PUSH, EVERYONE! PUSH!"

They pushed the bed down the street
and over the hill.

The bed went faster and faster.

It roared out of town.

It plowed through a pumpkin patch

and bounced into the farmer's yard.

The old lady stepped off the bed.

The porch light came on.

"The farmer's coming!" said Minnie.

"Push!" whispered Moo.

When the farmer came out
the lady pointed her cane at him.
"What kind of bus company
are you running here, mister?"
"What?" said the farmer.
"Does this look like Fifth Street?"
said the little old lady.

The Dream

The bed squeaked up the hill.

"We're almost there," said Moo.

The animals pushed.

"Just a little farther," said Minnie.

They pushed and pushed.

Slowly, the bed squeaked to a stop

under the old oak tree.

"Thank goodness," said Madge.

She flopped onto the bed.

"You said it!" moaned Bea.

"Move over," said Hamlet.

The sheep squeezed onto the bed.

Soon they were all snoring.

Minnie and Moo lay down

under the old oak tree.

Moo gave Minnie a pillow

and tucked her in

under a warm blanket.

"Sweet dreams," she said.

Minnie clutched her bag of treats.

"Mmmm," she mumbled.

The Halloween moon looked down
from high above the old oak tree.
Far away, a dog howled
and a dream came in the night . . .
a chocolate dream.